A GIFT FOR:

_____

FROM:

_____

Story time and play time are a lot more fun when You're The Star!

Story time

1. Put on the cape and secure it around your shoulders.

2. Turn the medallion to ON using the switch located on its side.

3. Press the front of the medallion one time to begin story time!

- *When an adult reads the highlighted phrases in the book, you'll hear music, voices, and other sounds.*

Play time

1. Put on the cape and secure it around your shoulders.

2. Turn the medallion to ON using the switch located on its side.

3. Press the front of the medallion two times to begin play time!

- *Say the trigger phrases listed in the back of each book to hear more sounds and to make play time even more fun!*

Collect all of Princess Harmony's books to find out more magical phrases!

Copyright © 2013 Hallmark Licensing, LLC

Published by Hallmark Gift Books,
a division of Hallmark Cards, Inc.,
Kansas City, MO 64141
Visit us on the Web at Hallmark.com.

Editorial Director: Carrie Bolin
Editor: Nate Barbarick
Art Director: Jan Mastin
Designer: Brian Pilachowski
Production Designer: Bryan Ring

ISBN: 978-1-59530-957-0
KOB1064

Printed and bound in China
JUL13

PRINCESS
HARMONY
AND THE MISSING INSTRUMENTS

BY AMY TROWBRIDGE-YATES

ILLUSTRATED BY KARLA TAYLOR

Hallmark

Princess Harmony considered herself to be one lucky princess. The magical cape Queen Nana had given her let her talk to animals in the forest, and *they* could talk to *her*.

But that wasn't even the best part! Her animal friends loved music and dancing just as much as she did. So they spent their days playing together, to the delight of all the woodland animals. Harmony was so happy to be the Royal Princess of the Forest.

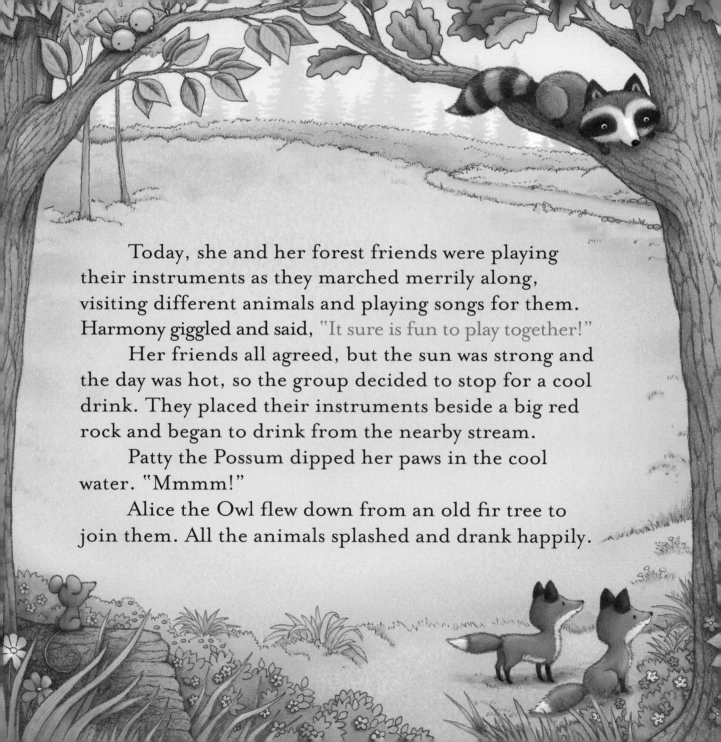

Today, she and her forest friends were playing
their instruments as they marched merrily along,
visiting different animals and playing songs for them.
Harmony giggled and said, "It sure is fun to play together!"

Her friends all agreed, but the sun was strong and
the day was hot, so the group decided to stop for a cool
drink. They placed their instruments beside a big red
rock and began to drink from the nearby stream.

Patty the Possum dipped her paws in the cool
water. "Mmmm!"

Alice the Owl flew down from an old fir tree to
join them. All the animals splashed and drank happily.

Feeling much cooler and ready to play again, Princess Harmony called to the group, "I have an idea! Let's go play a song for the bears."

But instead of gathering their instruments, the animals stood by the big red rock in amazement. Simon let out a skunky squeal. "Our instruments are gone!"

And they were. They certainly weren't where they had left them.

Henry the Hedgehog buried his head in his paws. "Oh no! What will we do without music?"

"They've got to be here somewhere," Harmony said. "Let's figure this out!"

She began searching all around the big red rock. The animals joined in, looking nearby, but no one found any sign of the instruments.

They searched the bushes. Still nothing. Harmony searched in the fallen trees, but she was stumped. Their instruments were just nowhere to be found.

Simon's skunk lip began to tremble. "Will we ever find our instruments, Princess Harmony?"

Harmony sat down on a bumpy log and patted Simon's shoulder. "I don't know, Simon," she admitted. "But we haven't looked everywhere yet."

"This just makes no sense!" said Hip. "What, did my drum just hop away?"

"For once, I agree with Hip," said Hop. "Somebunny must know something!"

Suddenly, they heard the flapping of wings. A small bluebird landed on Harmony's knee.

"Did I hear that you've lost your instruments?" the bird asked excitedly.

"Yes! We've been searching for them." said Simon.

"I can help you," said the bird. "I just saw the beaver with a bunch of instruments down by the lake. Follow me, and I'll show you!"

The animals raced to follow the bluebird. Patty's possum legs ran faster than they'd ever run before, and Hip and Hop couldn't jump-jump-jump quickly enough!

At last, they came to the lake at the far end of the forest and saw a beaver sticking Simon Skunk's keyboard into the dam he was building. But that wasn't all—Alice's tambourine, Hip and Hop's drums, Henry's trombone, and even Patty's flute were jammed between sticks, leaves, and mud.

A dam built out of their instruments? The animals weren't so sure about this.

The group walked closer, and the beaver smiled proudly at them. "How do you like my dam?" he asked them. "Pretty fancy, huh?"

"Well," said Harmony, "it is unique, but those fancy things in there are our instruments."

Beaver looked at her, then at the instruments, not understanding.

"We use them to play songs!" she explained.

But Beaver didn't believe Harmony—he thought they were excellent materials for his dam. And he liked how shiny some of them were.

"Fiddlesticks!" said Harmony. "We need our instruments back, please. After all, what would we do without music?"

Beaver didn't know much about music, but he
did know that there were some things you couldn't do
without—like sticks and mud.

"Here you go," he said, pulling the instruments
free and wiping off the mud and leaves. "Sounds like
you need these more than I do. But will you show me
how you use them?"

Harmony jumped up and down as the animals
excitedly began to play a little ditty.

Enjoying the music, Beaver closed his eyes and began to slap his large, flat tail in excitement. *Boooom-Boom! Boooom-Boom!* It made a nice, deep, rhythmic sound.

"You have a built-in instrument!" cried Harmony. "Slap your tail a little faster!"

The animals smiled at one another as they played with Beaver's beat. Henry had to stop playing a few times so he could laugh. Alice swooped down and around the merry band, shaking her tambourine.

Harmony danced and twirled between her friends before pulling them along through the forest. She took Beaver's paw and laughed. "It sure is fun to play together!"

Turn the page for more fun with Princess Harmony!

Press the medallion one more time,
then try saying these phrases
when you're out playing!

I'm the princess!

Oh, fiddlesticks!

Play my song!

I love you!

Let's have a ball!

 NEW

Time to dance!

Charmed, I'm sure

Discover even more fun phrases in other Princess Harmony books!

If you have enjoyed
Princess Harmony's adventure,
we would love to hear from you.

Please send your comments to:

Hallmark Book Feedback

P.O. Box 419034

Mail Drop 215

Kansas City, MO 64141

Or e-mail us at:

booknotes@hallmark.com